ALMA

and How She Got Her Name

Juana Martinez-Neal

CANDLEWICK PRESS

Alma Sofia Esperanza José Pura Candela had a long name—

too long, if you asked her.

"My name is so long, Daddy. It never fits," Alma said.

"Come here," he said. "Let me tell you the story of your name. Then you decide if it fits."

Sofia

was your grandmother," he began. "She loved books, poetry, jasmine flowers, and, of course, me. She was the one who taught me how to read."

"I love books and flowers . . . and you, too, Daddy!"

I am

Sofia

ESPERANZA was your great-grandmother," he continued. "She hoped to travel, but never left the city where she was born. Her only son grew up to cross the seven seas. Wherever her sailor son went, so did Esperanza's heart."

"The world is so big! I want to go see it, Daddy.
You and me together."

I am

ESPERANZA

JOSÉ was my father," Alma's daddy said. "He was an artist with a big family, like many people had back then. Early each morning, he walked to the mountains and the plazas to paint everyday life. Sometimes I went along. Your grandfather taught me to see and love our people."

"I wake up early every day, and I draw a lot, too!
This morning, I drew a kitty cat for you, Daddy!"

I am

JOSÉ

Pura was your great-aunt. She believed that the spirits of our ancestors are always with us, watching over us. When you were born, she tied a red string around your wrist: a charm to keep you safe."

Candela

was your other grandmother.
She always stood up for what was right."

"I love the story of my name! Now, tell me about *Alma*, Daddy. Where does that come from?"

"I picked the name *Alma* just for you. You are the first and the only Alma. You will make your own story."

"That's my name, and it fits me just right!
I am Alma, and I have a story to tell."

A Note from Juana

My name is Juana Carlota Martinez Pizarro. My father named me *Juana* after his mother, Juana Francisca. My mother chose the name *Carla* to honor the memory of her uncle, Carlos. My father was a man of decisions, so when it was time to register my birth, he changed *Carla* to *Carlota* on the birth certificate. He was convinced that *Juana Carlota* was the mighty name he wanted for his daughter. Thanks to that change, I got stuck with what I thought was the most old-fashioned, harsh, ugly, and way-too-Spanish name in all of Lima, Peru, where I grew up! Little did I know that later on, after I moved to the United States, it would feel unique and remind me every day of where I come from.

What is the story of your name?
What story would you like to tell?

To Victor Nicolás Martínez Gómez, my dad

First edition 2018

Library of Congress Catalog Card Number pending
ISBN 978-0-7636-9355-8 (English hardcover)
ISBN 978-0-7636-9358-9 (Spanish hardcover)

18 19 20 21 22 23 CCP 10 9 8 7 6 5 4 3 2 1

Printed in Shenzhen, Guangdong, China

This book was typeset in Youbee.
The illustrations were done with graphite, colored pencils,
and print transfers on handmade textured paper.

Candlewick Press
99 Dover Street
Somerville, Massachusetts 02144

visit us at www.candlewick.com